Are you brave enough
to come into
the Wilderness?

The moment you step across
the boundary,
you'll be changed forever . . .

Derelict → House

Grotto

Lily Pond

Dragon Gardens

Witch's Hut ♥

Valley of ller Plants

Swamp

Skull Rock

Raven's Garden

For Wild Justice, for giving a voice to the Wild Things.—G.L.

To everyone in my old gang who used to camp out in
the Chalk Pits. And all those other good times.—R.B.

OXFORD
UNIVERSITY PRESS

Great Clarendon Street, Oxford OX2 6DP
Oxford University Press is a department of the University of Oxford.
It furthers the University's objective of excellence in research, scholarship,
and education by publishing worldwide. Oxford is a registered trade mark
of Oxford University Press in the UK and in certain other countries

Text copyright © Gill Lewis 2021
Illustrations copyright © Rebecca Bagley 2021

The moral rights of the author have been asserted

Database right Oxford University Press (maker)

First published 2021

British Library Cataloguing in Publication Data

Data available

ISBN 978-0-19-277178-0

1 3 5 7 9 10 8 6 4 2

Printed in China

Paper used in the production of this book is a natural,
recyclable product made from wood grown in sustainable forests.
The manufacturing process conforms to the environmental
regulations of the country of origin.

Willow Wildthing
and the
Magic Spell

Written by Gill Lewis

Illustrated by Rebecca Bagley

OXFORD
UNIVERSITY PRESS

Chapter 1
The Wizard and
The Cloak of Lies

'CAW! CAW! CAW!'

Willow woke up to the loud cawing of a crow outside. It was still dark. She glanced at her alarm clock and the bright red numbers showed 3.40 a.m. It was very early morning. Too early for the birds, but a crow was definitely cawing loudly. Willow's dog Sniff sat up at the end of her bed, his ears pricked and listening too.

1

Then Willow heard the patter of feet in the hallway and her bedroom door creaked open.

'Noisy bird,' said Freddie.

Freddie was Willow's little brother. He was three years old, and now that he was in a big bed, he often wandered about if he woke up at night.

'Noisy bird,' agreed Willow.

'Caw! Caw!' said Freddie.

Willow laughed. 'Caw! Caw!'

'CAW! CAW! CAW! CAW! CAW!' cawed the crow outside.

Willow frowned. What was a crow making such a noise about in the darkness?

Willow picked up Sniff, climbed out of bed and walked to the open window. Freddie climbed up on a chair to look out too. The silver light from the moon lit up the tops of the trees in the patch of woodland beyond the garden. It had once been the gardens and grounds of an old house. The house had burned down and fallen into ruin long ago and the gardens had grown wild, while roads and houses and shops had grown around them. Now it was a small patch of green in the middle of the grey town. Willow knew it as the Wilderness. She loved the Wilderness more than anywhere. It was the place she had adventures with her friends, the Wild Things. It was where time and distance stretched and where anything could happen.

'I'll take you to the Wilderness one day, Freddie,' said Willow. 'I promise.'

'CAW! CAW!'

Willow looked out into the darkness and a low growl rose up in Sniff's throat.

'What is it, Sniff?' she said.

The path at the end of the garden was lit by a single street lamp, and in its pool of light, Willow could see the crow swooping up and down as if it were trying to dive-bomb something.

'Grrrr . . .' growled Sniff.

Then Willow saw a figure on the other side of the path inside the Wilderness. The figure was tall and seemed to be wearing a long overcoat. It was going from tree to tree, stopping at each one.

The crow was definitely trying to attack, because the figure kept flinging its arms about, to keep it away.

'Bad wizard,' whispered Freddie.

Willow nodded. The figure did look a bit like the evil wizard in a book Willow had read to Freddie the night before. The story had been called the Cloak of Lies. The wizard had worn a cloak of darkness that hid everything, including the truth. He had slunk around in the shadows too.

The figure disappeared further into the Wilderness and was gone, followed by the crow's angry cries.

A chill wind curled in through the window and Willow shivered and climbed back into bed. 'Back to bed, Freddie,' she said. But she had already guessed that Freddie would climb in bed beside her. She folded her arms around him, hugging him tightly and Sniff settled himself at their feet.

Outside the sky began to lighten, and

the stars began to fade. And as they did, birdsong rose up from the Wilderness; bubbling chirrups, high-pitched twitters, warbling melodies, and the soft cooing of doves.

'Listen to that,' whispered Willow. 'It's the dawn chorus. The birds are singing just for us.'

But Freddie was already asleep, his gentle snoring in time with the cooing of the doves. Willow closed her eyes and tried to sleep but the image of the figure she had seen worried her. Who was he? And why had he been going from tree to tree? And as Willow fell into sleep, the dark wizard walked through her dreams. He was hiding in the shadows, laughing at her, swirling his black Cloak of Lies.

Chapter 2
Silence of the Birds

Willow woke to bright sunlight. She looked at her clock again and it was nine o'clock. She could hear Freddie downstairs banging his spoon on the table demanding breakfast.

'Uff!' woofed Sniff. He thought it was time Willow should get up too.

Sniff was Willow's dog. No one had wanted him at the rescue centre. He was a small scruffy dog with one eye and wonky teeth, but the moment Willow had seen him, she just knew they had to be together.

'Uff!' woofed Sniff again.

Willow climbed out of bed and walked over to the window to see if the crow or the figure were still there, but there was no one except for a dog walker further down the path. But something was different. Then Willow noticed it, and it made her feel cold inside. Some of the taller trees in the Wilderness had bright fluorescent orange crosses on their tree trunks. The cloaked figure had painted the orange crosses in the night.

She went downstairs into the kitchen. Mum was getting Freddie's breakfast ready and Dad was filling the dishwasher. The TV was on with the sound turned down and Freddie was watching a cartoon.

'This is Freddie's second breakfast,' Mum beamed. 'He's getting better every day.'

Willow smiled too. Freddie had been poorly since he had been born and sometimes needed to stay in hospital. It's why they had moved from their old town to be closer to the hospital. But as Freddie was getting older, he was getting stronger too and didn't need to spend as much time in hospital.

Willow sat down at the table and poured herself some orange juice. 'What are those orange crosses on the trees?' she asked.

Dad looked outside. 'I hadn't noticed them before. I'm not sure. Trees are sometimes marked if they need to be taken down.'

Willow frowned. 'Why do trees need to

be taken down?'

'Well, they can be dangerous if they fall on cars or buildings,' said Dad.

'But those trees are in a wood,' said Willow. 'They can't fall on anything like that. I hope no one is thinking of taking them down.'

'Bad wizard,' said Freddie.

Willow looked at him, but Freddie was pointing at the TV screen. The programme had changed from cartoons to local news, and there was a tall man in a long dark overcoat. There was something familiar about him. He did look a bit like the figure she has seen last night.

'That's Lord Smog,' said Mum. 'He's a local property developer.'

'What's a property developer?' asked Willow.

'Someone who buys up land to build houses,' said Mum. 'He owns Smog Homes. He builds all around the town.'

'He's very rich,' said Dad.

'How rich?' said Willow.

'Richer than rich,' said Dad.

Willow stared at the man on the screen and wondered how rich some people wanted to be.

The news finished with a weatherman

pointing at bright sunshine.

'It's going to be a lovely day,' said Mum, opening the doors to the patio. Sniff ran outside barking and chasing a butterfly up the garden path.

Birdsong flowed into the house.

'That's a blackbird,' said Willow.

'How do you know?' said Mum.

'I've been watching it,' said Willow. 'And further down the garden there's a robin singing.'

'It's a lovely sound,' said Mum, sipping her tea. 'It reminds me of summer when I was little.'

But just then, another sound tore through the air. It ripped the peace of the morning apart. A mechanical, whizzing, grinding came from the far side of the Wilderness.

13

Freddie covered his ears, and Willow ran to the window.

'What's making that noise?' shouted Willow above the din.

'Sounds like a chainsaw,' said Dad.

'A chainsaw?' said Willow. She felt sick inside. 'A chainsaw for cutting trees?'

'I guess so,' said Dad.

The sound abruptly stopped and was replaced by a creaking, then a thundering crash as birds flew up into the air.

Somewhere on the other side of the Wilderness a tree had just fallen.

A moment of silence followed.

A deathly hush.

Nothing made a sound.

Even the birds stopped singing.

Chapter 3
Marked with an X

Panic filled Willow.

The Wilderness was in trouble. She had to find her friends, the Wild Things, and go and stop whoever was cutting down the trees.

'I've got to go,' said Willow.

'Where?' said Mum.

'I'm going to Raven's house to see my friends,' she called as she ran out into the garden.

'Don't be long,' shouted Mum.

But Willow was already racing down
the garden with Sniff at her heels. She
slipped under the hedge and ran along the
path towards Raven's house at the end of
the street, but Raven and four other figures
were pulling a plank across the Green Slime
River, the watery ditch between the path and
the Wilderness.

Her friends; Raven, Fox, Hare, Bear,
and Mouse were the Wild Things she had
adventures with in the Wilderness. Outside
of the Wilderness they were children, but
the Wilderness had a curious effect on them.
They became wilder, somehow. Feral.

'You're here already!' said Willow.

'Did you hear it too?' said Raven.

'Yes,' said Willow. 'And look at all these
trees marked with an X. It means they're

going to be chopped down too.'

'We have to stop them,' said Hare.

'Who are they?' said Mouse.

'I don't know,' said Fox, 'but we're going to find out.'

The Wild Things pulled their shoes off and left them under a bush. To go barefoot was one of the rules of the Wilderness. Willow could see the others become a bit wilder. Fox became more foxy. Raven's cloak fell around her like wings, the frayed edges becoming feathers. Hare bounced up and down on her long legs and Bear scratched his stomach.

Mouse twitched his nose. 'Come on, there's no time to lose.' He scuttled away into a tunnel made from thorns and brambles. The Holloway was the secret entrance to the Wilderness.

Willow followed her friends, crawling on hands and knees until they were on the other side, at the top of a steep slope. Below them, River Camp lay in the bend of the river. It was their den made from branches and an old tarpaulin. There was a ring of stones around a campfire where they made hot chocolate and toasted marshmallows. River Camp was their special place where they read books, drew maps, and planned adventures. The Wilderness was the best place in the world.

The grinding mechanical noise started again, and Willow looked at the others. 'Another tree is going to fall.'

'We'll have to follow the sound,' said Raven.

Just then, Sniff sniffed the air and barked. He began wagging his tail and bounded up to a small bush that seemed to have magically appeared on the top of the slope next to the Wild Things.

Willow peered more closely. 'Hazel, is that you?'

The bush shook a few branches away and a girl stood before them. Two other bushes stepped out from behind the trees. Two boys emerged. Their faces were

camouflaged with mud and bits of leaf and moss.

'Rowan and Ash,' said Mouse. 'You're here too.'

They were the Barkskins, another tribe the Wild Things had met before. They lived in a tree house in the Ogre Tree. It was the oldest tree in the forest.

'Have you heard?' said Hazel. The mud beneath her eyes was wet and it looked like she had been crying. 'They're cutting down the forest.'

'Who are?' said Hare.

'We don't know,' said Ash.

'We saw them this morning on the other side of the forest. They're cutting down the trees marked with an X.'

'Can you show us?' said Bear.

Hazel nodded. 'Follow us.'

The Wild Things ran with the Barkskins, their feet flying over the twisted roots until they reached the Barkskins' den in the Ogre Tree. The Ogre Tree was a huge yew tree, with roots like clawed feet. It was over a thousand years old.

'Look!' said Hazel. She pointed to an orange X. 'Someone has marked the Ogre tree to be chopped. If this tree is chopped down, then no others are safe.'

'I saw someone marking other trees,' said Willow. 'A figure cloaked in black was in the Wilderness early this morning.'

'It sounds like the man we saw at the edge of the forest where the first tree was chopped down,' said Ash. 'Come on, we'll show you.'

The Barkskins led the way through the trees to the other side of the Wilderness. The Wild Things hadn't been to the far side of the Wilderness before. Beyond the line of trees were office blocks and a garage selling shiny cars.

'Look,' said Hazel, coming to a stop. 'They've put nets over the trees and put up tall fences to stop people coming in.'

'Why do they put nets over the trees?' asked Fox.

'They're not allowed to cut down trees with nests,' said Hazel, 'so they stop the birds nesting.'

'But then there'll be no birds,' said Bear.

'And no birdsong,' said Willow.

'Look,' said Mouse. 'Is that the person you saw?'

On the other side of the fencing, outside the Wilderness, a tall man in dark overcoat was talking to two men in yellow hard hats. They were standing by a large truck they were filling with cut logs. Beside the truck was a row of yellow diggers.

The Wild Things and the Barkskins followed Willow further forward.

'Yes, it is,' said Willow. 'It's Lord Smog, the property developer.'

Lord Smog turned to look at Willow and

25

the other children. 'Hey, you!' he called. 'No one's allowed in there. It's private property.'

Hazel marched forward. 'Stop cutting down the trees,' she shouted.

'And let the birds build their nests,' agreed Raven, standing beside her. The wings of her cape caught the breeze and flared out behind her.

'These are our woods,' said Bear.

Lord Smog took a step towards them. 'That's where you are wrong,' he said, slowly looking at each of them in turn. 'This land belongs to me. I bought it from the council. So, you are trespassing.'

Hare glanced at a large sign behind Lord Smog. It was a huge billboard showing new houses. *Smog Homes. Crows' Nest Housing.* 'You can't build here. If you take

down the trees there'll be no nests or birds.'

'You have to go back to your homes,' said Lord Smog. 'This is now a building site. We can't have children running about. It's not safe.' He pointed to a tall ash tree next to them which was marked with a cross. 'That one is the next to be cut down.'

'We won't let you chop the trees,' said Hazel.

'Never,' said Raven.

Hare stared at the cut stump of a tree. 'You can't cut the trees. It hurts the forest. The other trees know their friends are being killed.'

Lord Smog sneered. 'You are a very silly girl aren't you. They're just trees.'

Mouse blew a raspberry at him because it seemed the right thing to do.

Lord Smog pulled out his phone. 'If you don't leave now, I'm calling the police.'

'Come on,' said Fox to the others, 'we'll find a way to stop him.'

The Wild Things followed the Barkskins back to the Ogre Tree.

Willow shivered as she walked beneath the trees. They seemed darker somehow. She wondered if Hare could be right, if trees did know other trees in the forest were being cut down.

'We're going to stay up in our tree house and refuse to move,' said Hazel.

Ash pulled out his phone. 'I'm going to email the local newspaper and tell them we're holding a protest. We're not going to let Lord Smog cut down the oldest tree in the town.'

Rowan nodded in agreement and turned to

the Wild Things. 'You can join us too.'

'But it won't stop them cutting the other trees,' said Bear.

'What else can we do?' said Ash.

Raven frowned. 'There must be a way to stop Lord Smog.'

'I know who we could ask,' said Fox. 'She's helped us before.'

Raven nodded and turned to the other Wild Things. 'Let's go and find the witch.'

Chapter 4
The Money Wizard

'CAW! CAW!'

The witch's crow bobbed up and down on a branch as the Wild Things approached the witch's hut. The witch had helped them before and they hoped she could help them now.

The crow flew down to rest on a pile of boxes stacked outside the hut.

At first it looked as if the witch was out, but a loud crash and the sound of china breaking came from inside.

'Hello?' said Willow knocking at the door.

'Wait a minute,' came the reply.

'CAW!' said the crow.

The hut door swung open and the Wild Things looked inside. The witch's hut looked different. All the pictures had been taken down from the walls. The books were piled into more boxes, and a washing up bowl held cups and plates.

'Are you leaving us?' said Mouse.

The witch turned around. Her eyes were red, and she blew her nose into a large spotted hanky. 'Haven't you heard? We all have to leave. The Wilderness has been bought and is going to be turned into new houses.'

'We know,' said Fox. 'That's why we came to you. We throught you might be able to help.'

'We thought you could put a spell on Lord Smog,' said Mouse. 'Make him stop.'

The witch frowned. 'I wish I could put a spell on him. He's a horrible man.'

'I saw him in the Wilderness early this morning,' said Willow.

'I did too,' said the witch. 'Crow here kept trying to chase him away.'

'Lord Smog said he'd call the police if we didn't leave,' said Bear.

'It's what he said to me too,' said the witch. 'He came here to tell me. He said I have until sunset to remove my things.'

'So why can't you put a spell on him?' said Hare.

'The witch pulled out a rickety chair and sank down onto it. 'I'm not a real witch, you know that. I'm just a writer.'

Hare took a step back. 'But there's magic in here,' she said. 'You said so yourself.'

'There is,' agreed the witch. 'It's just many people don't seem to be able to see that. Or they forget how to. I've been coming here for years. Since I was a child

actually. I played here with my friends too. I grew up watching the houses and roads being built up around this place. I suppose I knew it was always going to happen here one day. I just hoped I wouldn't be here to see it.'

'So you're just giving up?' said Raven.

'You don't know Lord Smog,' said the witch. 'There's nothing that can stop him.'

'We can't give up,' said Fox.

'River Camp is our home,' said Bear. 'Where else will we toast marshmallows?'

'Where else will the birds live?' said Raven.

'Where else can we play?' said Hare. 'I don't have a garden at home.'

Mouse sat down and put his head in his hands. 'This is the best place in the world. It's my happy place.'

'I promised Freddie I would bring him here,' said Willow. 'We won't give up.'

'You have to,' said the witch sharply. 'I know Lord Smog. He always gets his own way. Forget your spells and go home. Words won't do anything. Lord Smog is called the money wizard. And there's nothing that speaks more powerfully than money.'

Chapter 5
Arrow to the Heart

Willow followed the other Wild Things out of the Wilderness. They stood on the path that ran behind the gardens. The air was filled with the roar of a chainsaw. Even Sniff seemed subdued. He lay down at Willow's feet and put his head in his paws.

'We can't go back, ever,' said Mouse.

'We can still all be friends,' said Fox. 'Nothing can change that.'

'It's not the same,' said Hare. 'There'll be

nowhere to go. Nothing to do.'

'I'm hungry,' said Bear. 'I want to be back at River Camp toasting marshmallows.'

'Come to mine,' said Raven. 'We can make a den in my garden.'

Sniff whined and pawed at Willow.

'I'm going home first,' said Willow. 'I'll come over later.'

Willow crawled under the hedge with Sniff and went into the house. Willow felt a knot of worry in her chest when she saw Mum and Dad talking to a police officer in the hallway.

'There you are,' said Mum. 'I was coming to find you.'

The woman officer smiled at Willow. 'I'm a community officer making sure that no

one goes into the grounds of the old house. There's going to be development work and it will be dangerous to play there. Lord Smog has reported seeing children in there today. He's concerned for their safety.'

'But what about the safety of all the animals that live in there,' Willow blurted out. 'He can't just chop all the trees down.'

'People need homes to live in,' said Dad.

'But the animals do too,' said Willow. 'Why does Lord Smog think he can just take animals' homes away. We have to stop him.'

'Lord Smog brings a lot of jobs to the community,' said Dad.

'He just wants money,' said Willow.

Mum sighed. 'It's not up to us to tell him what to do.'

'Why not?' said Willow. 'Who else is going to stop him?'

The police officer smiled sympathetically. 'The land belongs to Lord Smog. He's allowed to build there.'

'You can't go in there, any more,' said Mum. 'Promise me.'

But Willow felt furious tears burn in her eyes. She turned and went into the sitting room where Freddie was playing with his bricks. She sat down beside him and let her tears fall. 'I can't take you into the Wilderness, Freddie,' she said. 'I can't go there ever again.' She felt her heart ache for the place she loved but would lose. She would never see River Camp in the bend in the river. She would never visit the secret garden and watch the pond dragons wriggle to the depths of the green pools. She would never sit with her friends around the campfire listening to Hare's stories, while the wood smoke drifted up on the warm summer evenings. The trees were being chopped down and the diggers were lined up to flatten the Wilderness. She couldn't stop Lord Smog. No one could. Not even Mum or Dad seemed to care what happened.

Big aching sobs built up inside her.

Freddie stood up and put his arms around her.

'I'm sorry, Freddie,' she cried.

'Sad?' said Freddie.

Willow nodded. 'I'm sad.'

'I love you,' said Freddie.

Willow smiled through her tears. 'You always say things that make me feel better,' she said, drying her eyes. 'How do you do it?'

'Magic words,' laughed Freddie.

'Magic words?' said Willow.

Freddie nodded. 'Magic.'

'Yes,' said Willow. 'You're right, Freddie. You're a genius. Words can be magic. You've given me a brilliant idea.' She stood up and Sniff bounded next to her, as if he knew exactly what she was about to do. 'I've got to go, Freddie. But I'll be back. And I'll take you to the Wilderness soon, I promise.'

Willow grabbed her small backpack and stuffed pencils and pens inside, and sheets of paper, then ran down the end of the garden.

She slipped under the fence and sprinted to Raven's house at the end of the street. Raven and the other Wild Things were sitting on the grass. They had started making a den, but it lay half-made on the ground.

Fox looked up. 'We're not making a den any more. It can never be the same as River Camp.

'You have to come with me,' said Willow. 'I think there might be a way to save the Wilderness.'

'How?' said Raven scrambling to her feet.

'There's no time to explain here,' said Willow. 'We need to see the witch before she leaves the Wilderness for good.'

The Wild Things followed Willow and Sniff across the Green Slime River and into the

Wilderness. When they found the witch,
she was tying bags and boxes to her bicycle.

She looked up at them. 'You shouldn't be
in here.'

Mouse stepped forward. 'Willow knows
how to stop Lord Smog.'

'I've got an idea,' said Willow. 'Freddie
gave it to me.'

The witch shuffled past her.

'Well, I'd love to hear it, because I haven't come up with a way to stop him at all.'

'Let's make hot chocolate,' said Willow. 'This idea needs a bit of a plan.'

The witch bustled about lighting the campfire. The flames licked up around the cauldron of water and steam began to drift up into the air.

Willow sat down next to the other Wild Things around the fire. 'We have to make a powerful spell,' she said.

The witch shook her head. 'I told you, I'm not a witch. I don't do spells.'

Willow laughed. 'Yes you do. We all do.'

The witch frowned. 'I don't understand.'

'Well,' said Willow. 'What *is* a spell?'

Bear frowned. 'It's when we say certain words to make things happen.'

'Exactly,' Willow continued. 'Words are powerful. They can change the way we think. They can make us change what we do.'

'I don't think you'll change Lord Smog,' said the witch.

'We don't have to,' said Willow. 'We can change the minds of people who live around here. Make them stop him.'

'But how?' said Bear.

'We have to tell them about the
Wilderness,' said Willow. 'We have to tell
them about all the wild creatures in here.
We have to make them love it as much as
we do.'

The witch nodded. 'I think you're right.
We need them to be enchanted by this
place.'

'But we don't want people in here,' said
Raven, frowning. 'It's our secret.'

'It won't be for much longer,' said Willow.

Hare stared at the steam rising from the
hot water in the cauldron. She tried to hold
the mist in her hand, but it slipped through
her fingers into the air. 'But how do we find
which words to use? How do we write such

49

a powerful spell?'

The witch poured the hot water into mugs and stirred in chocolate powder. 'You have to make your listener love this place as much as you do. You have to make them *feel*. You have to make understand what they could lose.' She looked around at them all. 'You have to aim your spell, like an arrow to the heart.'

Chapter 6
The Wilderness Test

'But how do we start?' asked Fox.

The witch emptied out the cauldron of water and dried it with a towel. 'You start with one word,' she said. 'What's the first thing that comes into your head when you think of the Wilderness?'

'Birdsong,' said Willow.

'Dragons,' said Freddie.

'Starlight,' said Hare.

'River Camp,' said Fox.

'Marshmallows,' said Bear.

'Friends,' said Mouse.

'Freedom,' said Raven.

'Good,' said the witch. 'Now write them down and add more. It's like a potion. You need to give it time to stew.

Willow reached into her backpack and pulled out pens and paper and handed them around.

'Write from the heart,' said the witch. 'Don't try to make it clever or flashy. Write what you feel and put your words and thoughts into the cauldron and I'll stir it and stew it and I'll come up with a spell.'

Willow lay on her stomach in the dry leaves and chewed the end of her pen. It was hard to write why the Wilderness meant so much to her. It was everything. It was where she had learned to make a campfire, climb a tree, and watch the wild creatures that made it their home. It was vast and endless. So many stories and adventures lay waiting inside. She had learned to look after herself and her friends. It had begun the day she'd stood at edge of the Wilderness and taken off her shoes. Maybe that was the place to start. Maybe that was the way her parents had to see the Wilderness too. She put pen to paper and began to write the first words that popped into her head . . . *Shoeless, mud, oozing between toes, cool earth.*

The words swirled around in her mind and then she knew where to begin. She had to lead her parents barefoot into the wilderness too. She had to let them remember how it felt when they were

young. She put pen to paper and began
to write . . .

Come and meet me, in the place that is wild,
And remember how this felt, when you were
a child.
Where you can run barefoot, and thoughts
can fly free,
Where the world is as big as you want
it to be . . .

The Wild Things wrote in silence, only the
scratching of their pens and the birds singing
could be heard.

Only Mouse sat staring into space.

The witch leaned forward. 'Are you stuck?'

Mouse shook his head. 'I know what I want
to say. I just don't know how to write it.'

'Then tell me, and I'll write it down for you,' said the witch.

When they had finished, the Wild Things dropped their pieces of paper in to the empty cauldron and the witch swirled them around.

'Give me some time to make up a spell from your words,' she said. 'And come back with your parents and any adults you can find so that you can put your spell on them.'

'But how can we force them to come in here?' said Fox. 'Mine won't like this place. They love neat and tidy gardens.'

'My Dad's always working,' said Bear. 'He's never got any time.'

'I can't imagine my gran in here,' said Mouse. 'She hardly ever goes out of the house. She's scared of the outside.'

'So how do we make the adults come?' asked Hare.

'We give them no choice,' said Willow.

'We could refuse to come out,' said Raven, 'and hide in the trees with the Barkskins.'

Fox frowned. 'That'll just make them cross. We need to make them see the Wilderness like we do. Then they might help us stop Lord Smog.' He paced in circles. 'I have an idea that might work. But we need to make them come in here and find us. We need something to draw them in.'

'I know exactly what will draw mine in,' said Willow. 'But they won't like it.'

The witch finished her hot chocolate in

one gulp. 'I'm not sure I need to know.'

'Time for a Wild Squawk,' said Fox.

The Wild Things huddled together while the witch cleared up around them.

'What's your plan?' asked Raven.

Fox leaned forward. 'We need the adults to remember what it is to be wild. We need to make them Wild Things too.'

'How?' said Mouse.

Fox smiled. 'We set them a challenge. The Wilderness test.'

Chapter 7
Kidnap

The Wild Things headed back to River Camp.

'We'll need the Barkskins' help too,' said Fox.

'I'll go with Mouse and find them,' said Bear.

Hare sat down and pulled out the map, tracing a route through the Wilderness. Willow and Fox wrote letters to give to the adults to make sure they came.

'Ready?' said Willow, when Bear and Mouse returned.

Bear nodded. 'The Barkskins said they'll help us.'

'Come on then,' said Raven. 'This might be our only chance to save the Wilderness.'

Willow climbed up the slope to the Holloway and looked back. If their plan worked, they would come back to River Camp at sundown. If it worked, they could save the Wilderness. The thought of it being destroyed seemed unbearable.

A chainsaw roared into action on the far side of the Wilderness and Willow's heart sank knowing another tree was about to fall. She followed the others through the Holloway and out to the edge of the Wilderness.

They crossed the Green Slime River and
looked at each other.

'You know what you have to do,' said
Raven.

The others nodded.

'Can we bring food?' said Bear. 'I'm not sure I can do this without food.'

Raven nodded. 'I'll bring ingredients for explorer bread.'

'I'll bring jam,' said Hare.

'See you soon,' said Mouse.

They stood solemnly looking at each other. This was their only chance. Their last chance to save the place they loved most in the world.

Willow walked along the path with Sniff and slipped under the fence. Freddie was playing with his bricks on the grass and Mum was hanging out the washing.

'Where have you been?' said Mum.

'With friends,' said Willow.

'It's teatime,' said Mum. 'I've got some pasta on the boil.'

'Mum,' said Willow. 'Will you help me stop Lord Smog stop cutting down the trees?'

'What can we do?' said Mum. 'It's good building land. It'll be built on eventually.'

'Not if we try and stop it,' said Willow.

'No one's just going to let it stay wild,' said Mum. 'It's a mess. It's an eyesore.'

'You're wrong,' said Willow. 'It's beautiful. You just can't see it. You've forgotten how.'

Mum sighed. 'Willow, I haven't got time for this. Please bring Freddie in for tea in five minutes.'

Willow watched Mum go back into the house. She pulled out a piece of paper from her backpack and pegged it to the washing line. Then she knelt down beside Freddie. 'Do you want to go to the Wilderness, Freddie?'

'Dragons?' said Freddie.

Willow nodded. She had told Freddie the stories about the newts in the Land of the Dragon and about the lake where she had seen the shooting star. Freddie always wanted to go there with her.

Freddie put his arms up in the air for Willow to lift him up.

'Come on then,' she said. 'You can come with us.'

'Uff!' agreed Sniff, who seemed to think it the best idea.

Willow and Freddie scrambled under the garden fence and walked down the path hand in hand. Willow smiled. It felt good to be doing something. She couldn't just sit back and watch the Wilderness be destroyed.

The letter to her parents fluttered on the washing line in the breeze.

She knew every line by heart.

Dear Mum and Dad,

We have gone into the wilderness.
We may be some time.
You will have to tell Lord Smog that we are hiding
out in the woods and it will be too dangerous to
continue chopping trees.
We will not come back until the wilderness is saved.
If you want to find us, you will have to complete the
wilderness test.

Lots of love
Willow and Freddie

Challenge number 1: The Barefoot Test
Meet by the bridge across the Green Slime River
at 5 p.m.

(P.S. turn right along the path at the
bottom of the garden until you come
to a plank over the ditch)

'Come on, Freddie,' whispered Willow, as they took their shoes off and crossed over to the Wilderness. 'This will be like a big game of hide and seek.'

Freddie giggled and jumped up and down, his eyes wide with excitement.

Raven appeared from behind the trees. 'You made it. And you've got Freddie.'

'Yes,' Willow grinned. 'It was the easiest kidnap in the world.'

Chapter 8
Call of the Wild

The other Wild Things gathered on the edge of the Green Slime River. Hare was the last to come running along.

'I couldn't get away for ages,' said Fox. 'Mum and Dad are gardening and they wanted me to help. But I managed to slip away.'

'You've all left your letters?' Raven asked the others.

They nodded. They had all left the same letter as Willow, telling their parents and

Mouse's gran they had to gather here at 5 p.m.

'Do you think they'll come?' asked Mouse.

'They'll have to,' said Raven. 'We're trespassing on Lord Smog's land. He'll call the police.'

Bear scratched his tummy. 'I hope we don't get into trouble.'

'We're breaking the law,' said Fox.

Mouse's lip wobbled. 'Will we go to jail?'

'Just because it's a law doesn't make it right,' said Hare. 'Lord Smog is trespassing on the animals' land. Surely it's wrong that he's taking away their homes.'

'Come on, said Raven. 'We'll have to get to River Camp and make sure we've set up the challenges.'

The Wild Things scrambled through the Holloway. Mouse helped Freddie through and

stood beside him as he made his way down the steep root ladder.

'Welcome to the Wilderness, Freddie,' said Raven.

Freddie held onto Willow and looked shyly at the Wild Things.

'Right,' said Fox. 'Does everyone know where they are meant to be and what they are meant to do?'

The Wild Things nodded.

'It's time,' said Raven. She swirled her cloak of feathers. 'Let's go. And remember. Never give in.'

Willow stayed with Freddie and Bear at River Camp while the others set off across the Wilderness.

Raven was the one to start the challenge.

She crept back to the Green Slime River
and ducked down in the brambles. She
glanced at her watch. Nearly five o'clock.
She could hear footsteps coming from
both directions. She saw her mum and
Fox's mum and dad coming along the path.
Behind them came a tall man she guessed
was Hare's dad and then an older woman in

a pale lilac blouse and skirt that she thought might be Mouse's gran. From the other direction came Willow's parents followed by Bear's dad huffing along, looking cross.

'You got the letter too?' said Bear's dad to the other adults.

The other parents and Mouse's gran held up their letters.

'Willow's taken Freddie,' said Willow's mum. 'He's only three. There are streams and all sorts of dangers in there.'

'Highly irresponsible,' agreed Bear's dad. 'I don't have time for this. I'm meant to be working on an important report.'

'How do we get across?' asked Raven's mum.

Raven appeared on the other side of the Green Slime River. 'I'll lower the bridge, but first you have to take off your shoes and go barefoot.'

Bear's dad stepped forward. 'Is my son there too? It's time to stop playing games. You all need to come out of the woods now.'

'Yes,' said Fox's mum. 'We've had to notify the police to stop the tree cutting. Lord Smog isn't happy.'

'We're not happy either,' said Raven. 'Lord Smog is destroying the woods.'

'Please can you get Willow and her brother,' said Willow's Dad. 'It's past Freddie's bedtime.'

Raven shook her head. 'You have to complete the challenges.'

Raven's mum sighed. 'It's no good,' she said to the others. She kicked off her shoes and pulled off her socks. 'I know my daughter. She's not one to give in.'

'I'm not taking my shoes off,' said Fox's mum.

Raven shrugged her shoulders. 'Then I'll have to go.'

'Wait,' said Willow's mum. 'OK. If we take off our shoes will you take us to the others?'

'Eventually,' agreed Raven.

Hare's dad bent down and unlaced his boots. 'Right,' he said. 'The sooner we find them, the sooner we can get back. There's a football match I want to watch on TV.'

The other adults took off their shoes and socks and stood pressing their toes into the dry grass.

Mouse's gran stepped barefooted onto the grass. 'We're not going to get dirty, are we?'

Raven grinned. 'That's the plan,' she said. 'Taking your shoes off is challenge number one. Now we have to go into the Wilderness.'

The adults followed Raven, ducking down and crawling on their hands and knees through the Holloway. On the other side,

Raven led them away from the view of River
Camp and down to the edge of the Swamp.

'I'm covered in mud,' complained Fox's
dad.

'My skirt is ruined,' said Mouse's gran.

'Hi Gran,' called Mouse.

Gran looked across to an island in the
middle of the Swamp. Mouse was sitting on
the top of the rock.

'What are you doing up there?' called
Gran. 'Come back now.'

'I can't,' shouted Mouse. 'You'll have to
find a way to rescue me from Skull Rock.'

'It looks very boggy,' said Hare's dad. 'How
did you get across?'

'I can't remember,' said Mouse. 'But there's
a swamp monster that lives here.'

'Don't be silly,' said Gran. 'Come on. Time to go home.'

Raven stepped forward. 'He's not being silly. There is only one safe way across.' She pointed to a line of yellow flowers that marked a path across the swamp. Raven had placed them on the witch's secret sunken path that held their weight across the bog. 'You have to follow the flowers and do a little monster wiggle-dance in the middle of the bog or the bog monster will get you.'

'This is ridiculous,' said Bear's dad.

Hare's dad checked his watch. 'Look, can we just hurry up a bit.'

Bear's dad wagged his finger at Raven. 'This isn't a game. The police are on their way. It's time we all went home. I'm not doing a silly dance.' He strode out into the bog but began to sink deeper and deeper. He struggled and fell forward, his face splatting in the mud. 'Just look at me,' he roared.

Raven raised an eyebrow. 'I said the Bog Monster would get you.'

Mouse's gran couldn't help a giggle.

'It's NOT funny,' snapped Bear's dad.

Raven's mum held back a laugh. 'I'll help you out.' She waded out to help him but got stuck too, and it took the other adults to stand in a line and heave them all out.

'Where's Freddie?' said Willow's mum. 'This swamp isn't safe for a three-year-old to be around.'

'He's safe,' said Raven. 'You have to

cross the bog to find him.'

'And dance to the bog monster as you come over, or he'll get you,' said Mouse. 'Please Gran,' pleaded Mouse. 'Do it for me.'

'Just this once,' said Gran. She pottered across the bog following the flowers, her feet sinking a little way. She did a little wiggle halfway across.

Mouse stood up and clapped his hands. 'That was great Gran.'

'Well,' said Gran, walking to the other side, 'I was a bit of a dancer in my day.'

Raven's mum followed doing a little spin and a wiggle and joined Mouse and Gran.

'You go first,' said Willow's dad to Willow's mum.

'If we do it, we'll do it together, she said.

Willow's parents walked across the bog and did a mini monster wiggle.

All the adults did the monster wiggle, except for Bear's dad who grumbled and scowled his way across.

'Right,' he snapped. 'We've done with messing around. It's time to stop this nonsense.'

Raven grinned. 'Oh, but we've only just begun.'

Chapter 9
Wood Smoke and Memories

'Come on,' said Raven. 'We're off to the
Land of the Dragon.'

Mouse took Gran's hand in his and
smiled. 'I'm glad you came.'

Gran looked up at the towering trees.
'I suppose I had to. But I'm glad I did. I
haven't been in a wood for years. It sounds
silly, but I forgot how green it is. Quiet too.'

Willow's mum ran a hand through her
hair. 'Look,' she said, 'I really need to know

where Freddie is.'

'Willow has him,' said Raven.

'But there are dangerous things in here,' agreed Willow's dad. 'What if he fell in the bog?'

'This way,' said Raven. She led the way back across the bog and through an archway of branches.

'Where are we going?' asked Raven's mum.

'To the Land of the Dragon,' said Raven. She stopped beside a tall red-brick wall covered in ivy. She pulled away some branches to reveal two stone dragons and an old rotten door with flaking green paint. She knocked three times on the door and it swung open.

Fox stood on the other side.

'There you are,' said Fox's dad. 'Now, it really is time to get back. We're busy with the garden and I still haven't cut the grass.'

'Wait a minute,' said Fox's mum. She stepped through the door and looked around. 'What is this place?'

The door led to a garden that was surrounded by four tall red-brick walls. It was overgrown with brambles and ivy but had once been a walled garden. In the centre of the garden was a lily pond with a stone unicorn fountain that had stopped flowing long ago. At the far end of the garden was a grotto, an ornamental cave.

Fox's mum turned a full circle. 'Now this is a proper garden. It's beautiful. A garden lost in time.'

'Come and see the dragon,' said Fox,

taking her hand.

She followed Fox down some stone steps into the grotto. A shaft of light from the cave roof shone down onto a statue of a white dragon curled in a crystal pool.

Raven led the other parents to the lily pond. It was green with pondweed, but small creatures wriggled and swam in its depths.

Hare's dad leaned forward and peered in. 'Look, a newt. I haven't seen one since I was a boy. It's a long time since I've been pond dipping. I used to do it all the time.'

Fox's dad walked around looking up at the walls. 'I had no idea this was in here,' he said.

'How old is this place?' asked Fox's mum, when she came back out of the grotto. 'There's some history in here.'

'If you think this is old, you should come and meet the most ancient thing in the wilderness,' said Raven. 'It's over a thousand years old.'

Raven, Mouse and Fox led the adults through into the gloom of the Forest of Forever Night. Their feet slithered and slid on the dry pine needles.

Willow's mum shivered. 'It feels as if we're being watched,' she said.

They came to the clearing with a dark pool beside a huge tree.

Hare was standing beneath the tree.

'There you are!' said Hare's dad. 'I gave

you strict rules not to come in here. Besides, the football is starting soon.'

'It'll have to wait for once,' said Hare. 'We have to try to save this place. They can't just go chopping down all the trees.'

'New ones can be planted elsewhere,' said Hare's dad.

'You can never replace trees like these,' said Hare. She touched the trunk of a huge tree. 'It's a yew. It's the oldest tree here. It's over a thousand years old.'

'That is old,' said Fox's mum. 'Just imagine the history this tree has seen.'

'People forget how important trees are,' said Hare. 'They chop them down, forgetting they give us the air we breathe.'

'And cool shade,' said Mouse.

'They're home for animals,' said Fox. 'We

need trees.'

Hare stepped forward. 'Your challenge is to make a circle around the tree and join hands and say thank you to the tree for all that trees do.'

'I'm not doing that tree-hugging stuff,' said Bear's dad.

'I will,' said Gran, holding out her hand to the others. 'It can't hurt to hug a tree.'

So all the adults, except Bear's dad linked hands and stretched them around the tree.

'Thank you, tree,' said Gran, giving Mouse a little wink. 'Thank you for bringing Mouse to me.'

'Thank you,' said Raven's mum.

And after the thank yous there was a moment of silence as if the tree was listening.

Raven clapped her hands and three figures dropped out of the tree. 'Meet Hazel, Ash, and Rowan,' she said.

Hare's dad looked about. 'Where did you lot come from?'

'We're protesting,' Hazel said. 'We're staying up in our tree and we won't move until Lord Smog agrees to stop chopping down the trees.'

'Hazel is part of the next challenge,' said Hare. 'You have to have your faces painted with their mud before we go on.'

'I'm not doing that,' snapped Bear's dad. 'I really have important work to do. At least you can call my son and I'll take him home.'

Raven shook her head. You have to paint your face. She handed around Hazel's pot of mud.

Gran giggled as she rubbed it into her cheeks. 'It's probably good for the skin,' she said. 'People pay hundreds for this.'

'I'll have some after you, then,' said Raven's mum.

All the adults except for Bear's dad painted their faces with mud.

'There,' said Raven. 'You are part of the forest now. It's time to go to River Camp.'

Raven and Fox led the way out of the Forest of Forever Night, waving goodbye to the Barkskins who clambered back up into their tree. She looked back at the adults who were now covered in mud and bits of moss.

Bear's dad stomped close behind Raven and Fox, grumbling and tapping on his phone.

Suddenly he stopped.
'What is that
smell?' he said.

'What smell?' said
Raven.

'That smell,' said Bear's
dad. 'It reminds me of
something.'

Wood smoke drifted
through the air between the
trees. Somewhere a child
laughed, and a dog barked.

A smile crept across
Bear's dad's face. 'I haven't
smelt that for years.
It reminds me of my
childhood, camping out
with my dad and toasting

bread over a campfire. They were the best days spending time with him.' He closed his eyes and inhaled the smell. Remembering. 'I need to see my son,' he said urgently, opening his eyes. He looked around. 'Where is he? I want to share it with him too.'

Raven smiled. 'He's waiting for you by the campfire.'

And Bear's dad set off ahead of them, running through the trees, following the wood smoke and memories, to find his son.

Chapter 10
The Magic Spell

'There you are,' said Bear's dad.

Bear looked up from the campfire. 'Are you cross at me?'

'No, not at all,' said Bear's dad.

'But you've got work to do,' said Bear. 'You always have work to do.'

Bear's dad sat down by the fire. 'Work can wait. We should have done this a long time ago.'

Bear looked at his dad's muddy feet and

torn clothes. 'You look like one of us, a Wild Thing too.'

Bear's dad looked up and grinned. 'I'd forgotten how good it can be.'

'But where's Freddie?' said Willow's mum looking around and eyeing the river.

The tarpaulin of the den flew open. 'Boo!' said Freddie.

Sniff barked and Willow crawled out on her hands and knees following Freddie out of the den.

'There you both are,' said Willow's dad.

Willow's mum shook her head. 'I've been so worried.' She scooped Freddie up in her arms. 'You shouldn't have brought him here. There's rivers and steep slopes and deep bogs. Anything could happen.'

'But it didn't,' said Willow. 'It didn't,

because I was looking after him. I'm old enough now. Don't you trust me?'

'Freddie's' not been well,' said Dad. 'We have to be very careful with what we can let him do.'

'I know,' said Willow. 'But we can't wrap him in cotton wool forever. He has to live too.'

Bear's stomach grumbled very loudly. 'Sorry. But I'm really, really hungry.'

'Time for some explorer bread,' said Raven. 'She fetched the wet dough she'd made earlier and handed around sticks for everyone. She stuck a blob of dough on her stick and held it over the fire. The others did the same. Even Freddie did, and though Willow's mum looked a bit worried, she let Willow help him hold his stick in the fire.

The bread puffed up and turned from white to golden brown.

'Delicious,' said Willow's dad.

'CAW! CAW!' A crow flew down and settled next to Willow and Freddie. Their dad tried to shoo it away.

'Don't !' said Willow. 'That's the witch's crow.'

'The witch?' said Raven's mum.

A clanking and shuffling sound came from further up the slope and the witch emerged carrying a bag in one arm and a cauldron in the other. She eyed the Wild Things and the adults. 'Well it's quite a party here. I thought you might need some more mugs and I've brought some water for some nettle tea.'

'Nettle tea?' said Gran.

'Very good for you,' said the witch. 'You wouldn't think I was hundred and two.'

Gran peered at her. 'I'll have two cups of that then.'

'Now,' said the witch. 'Your final challenge is to listen to a spell the Wild Things have written for you.'

'A spell?' said Fox's dad.

The witch nodded. 'They gave me the words and I put them together. I think if you haven't been changed by coming in here, you will be by the end of this spell.' She handed a piece of paper to Willow. 'You each have a part to say.'

The Wild Things stood up in a circle around the adults and passed the spell from one to another as they read out the words.

'This is a spell for the wild,' said Willow, clearing her throat.

Willow;
Come and meet me, in this place that is wild,
And remember how it felt, when you were a
child.
Where you can run barefoot, and thoughts
can fly free,
Where the world is as big as you want it to be.

Bear;
Look up from your phone, look up, and see,
I'm here right now. Spend this time with me.
Tomorrow, I will no longer be small.
Tomorrow you'll wonder if you knew me
at all.

Fox;
So run with me, through this sun-dappled wood,
Ride dragons. Fight ogres. Be Robin Hood.
Test your fears and climb to the top of a tree,
And discover just how brave you can be.

Mouse;
Come with me, into this wild
place of mine,
Where dandelion seeds,
measure the time.
A small puff of air, they drift
up and away,
These are the best days of all,
the dandelion days.

Hare;

And walk with me, on a moon-bright
night,

Hear the nightingale's song, see an owl's
silent flight.

Look up and wonder, at the star-scattered
sky,

How did we come to be here . . . and why?

Raven;

Now sit by the campfire, in this place that
is wild,

Tell me your stories and stay for a while,

Stay in this place where adventure begins,

Open your heart, and let the wild in.

Willow;
Now imagine this place
without any trees,
Without any birds,
without any bees,
Imagine there is now
nowhere to play,
And nothing to do, day
after day after day.

Imagine that you have
to say to your child,
There is no place to
meet. There is no
place that is wild.

Chapter 11
The Wizard

When they had finished Willow folded the piece of paper.

The adults sat in silence. Bear's dad wiped a tear and said something about wood smoke in his eye.

'Thank you,' said Gran. 'That was beautiful. This place is beautiful.'

'I think we should make our garden wild like this,' said Fox's mum. 'It's magical.'

'I don't mind missing the football match,' said Hare's dad. 'This is much more fun.'

'I'm sorry we didn't trust you with Freddie,' said Willow's mum. 'We were worried, that's all.'

Willow smiled. 'So will you help us now?'

Raven's mum nodded. 'I can see why you want to save it.'

Willow's dad stood up and paced in circles. 'What if we set up a petition to raise money in the town to buy this place back and keep it as it is for everyone.'

'A bit late for that,' said a voice.

They all turned around.

Lord Smog and was coming through the trees, with two police officers. A TV crew was following close behind him. Lord Smog sneered down his nose at the Wild Things and the adults. 'This place belongs to me and you are all trespassing.'

Raven stood up. 'We're going to save it.'

Raven's mum folded her arms and glared at Lord Smog. 'And we're going to help them. It's time we have more space for kids to play and for wildlife too.'

The witch took a step towards Lord Smog. 'This place needs to be looked after for future generations. You should listen to the children.'

Lord Smog narrowed his eyes and peered at the witch. 'Oh dear me,' he said. 'It's Lydia isn't it! Still playing games in these woods after all these years.'

'Yes Reece, I'm still coming to the woods,' said the witch. 'I love them now as much as I did then.'

Willow looked between them. 'Do you know him?'

The witch nodded. 'Reece and I used to play in these woods a long time ago, didn't we?'

'Well you did,' said Lord Smog. 'I wasn't so keen on them myself,'

'But you came here didn't you,' said the witch. 'I was the one to catch you trying to steal birds' eggs. Crows' eggs weren't they?'

'CAW! CAW! CAW!' cawed the crow.

The Wild Things gasped. 'Did he take them?' said Hare.

'No,' said the witch, her eyes not leaving Lord Smog. 'Because I pushed him out of the tree. It was quite high up, if I recall.'

'And if I recall,' said Lord Smog, a smile

curling on his lips, your father said you had
to give me all your pocket money for a year
for breaking my arm.'

'Yes,' said the witch. 'But I stopped you
taking the eggs.'

Lord Smog laughed. 'Well there's nothing
you can do to stop me building houses here.'

'I know,' sighed the witch. 'And that's the
biggest injustice of all.'

The TV crew perked up. This was a
different angle on their story. 'We've already
met some kids in the woods who want to
save this place,' said the interviewer. 'But the
police had to send them home. Maybe we
can hear from you too.'

Lord Smog tried to wave them away.
'Police, please escort these people off my
land.'

'I'm afraid you'll have to leave,' said a police officer, or we'll have to arrest you.'

'Can we just have a quick interview for tonight's news?' said the interviewer.

The witch nodded and turned to Willow. 'Read out your spell like you did to us. Ask the viewers to come and save the Wilderness.'

So the Wild Things read out their spell and at the end Mouse declared it an emergency and told people to come and help.

Lord Smog tutted and interrupted, telling the interviewer that the homes were important and would bring jobs and business.

At the end of the interview the police asked everyone to leave the Wilderness by the end of the day, then they left with Lord Smog and the TV crew.

Willow sat back down and poked the fire sending sparks up into the evening air. 'This could be our last evening here,' she said.

'I wish spells really worked,' said Mouse. 'I wish we could stop Lord Smog.'

Raven's mum looked around the trees. 'I'm surprised it hasn't been built on already.'

'Maybe there is an ancient binding spell upon it,' said Raven. 'Maybe it's been kept secret until now.'

Hare nodded. 'Maybe Lord Smog is really a wizard and has found a way to break the binding spell.'

The witch stared hard at Hare and Mouse. 'Maybe you are right.' She started pacing circles round and round and round, tapping the side of her head to help her think. 'Binding spells cannot be broken. But they can be hidden, by a powerful spell of lies.'

'What do you mean?' said Willow.

The witch pulled
on her cloak tighter
around her. 'No time.
No time. You have
things to do and I
have things to do.
I have wizards to
fight. I will see you
tomorrow. There may
yet be a chance to
save the Wilderness.'

Chapter 12
The Binding Spell

Willow tossed and turned all night. Even Sniff decided it was more restful to sleep on the floor next to the bed rather than on the bed with Willow.

She had watched their interview on the TV and listened to their spell being broadcast. Then Lord Smog had said they were just naughty children playing in the wood, and that woods were very dangerous places. He himself had broken his arm in there as a child and didn't want that to happen to anyone else.

She turned over in bed to look at Sniff lying on the floor. 'If only spells worked, Sniff. It would be so much easier.'

'Uff!' woofed Sniff. His ears were pricked towards the window.

'What is it?' said Willow getting out of bed. She crossed to the window and looked out. She stared, her eyes becoming wider and wider and wider. 'Who are all those people, Sniff?'

Outside, all along the path between the garden and the Wilderness, was a line of people holding hands. Willow looked up and down the path, but the line of people went on and on and on.

A loud knocking came from the front

door and Willow could hear Dad letting Raven and her mum inside.

'Willow!' called Raven, bounding up to Willow's room. 'Have you heard?'

'What?'

'Our spell worked,' said Raven. 'People from the town listened to us last night on the TV and they've surrounded the Wilderness. They're not going to let Lord Smog onto his land.'

'Come on,' said Willow. 'We have to see this.'

Willow and Raven joined the other Wild Things at the path along the back gardens.

'We can't go into the Wilderness,' said Fox. 'We'll have to go all the way around the edge to the place where Lord Smog is trying to cut down trees.'

As the Wild Things ran, people cheered them when they recognized them from the news programme. At last they reached the diggers where Lord Smog was standing next to the town mayor and a line of police.

A police officer had a loudhailer and was asking the members of the public to move aside or arrests would be made. The mayor was nodding in agreement, his golden medals shining in the sun.

'CAW! CAW! CAW!'

A large crow flew out of the forest and swooped down on Lord Smog's head.

'CAW! CAW! CAW!'

'Get it away,' yelled Lord Smog.

A figure dressed in a black cloak walked out from the forest, a long staff in hand. Willow thought the witch had added a few

extra witchy things just for effect. The new pointed hat looked good too.

She lifted up a loudhailer of her own. 'It's time to stop this madness,' she yelled.

Lord Smog grabbed the loudhailer off a police officer while the crow pecked at his head. 'Call off your crow.'

'Crows have long memories,' said the witch. 'They pass it down through their families. They remember you were the one to try to steal their eggs in here as a boy.'

'Boooooo!' boooo-ed the crowd.

'Out of my woods,' shouted Lord Smog. 'Police, arrest this woman.'

The witch shook her head. 'All these people have come here today because they heard the children read a powerful spell. They want to save this place too.'

'You're still playing witch games, are you Lydia?' sneered Lord Smog.

'The children said there might be a binding spell on this land,' said the witch. 'And so I did a little research. It turns out there *is* something binding the protection of this space.'

Willow thought she saw Lord Smog shift uneasily. 'Get out of my woods,' roared Lord Smog.

The witch cackled a witchy cackle. 'I found that the day before you bought this land from the council, there was a fire in the mayor's office and some documents were destroyed. The police thought someone set the fire on purpose. That someone is in a lot of trouble.' She swivelled her glare to the mayor.

Sweat poured from the mayor's face. 'It wasn't my idea,' he shouted. He pointed his finger at Lord Smog. 'He made me do it,'

'Shut up,' snapped Lord Smog. 'You snivelling twit.'

The mayor puffed out his chest. 'I'm not a twit. And you haven't paid me the money for doing it yet.'

'The documents weren't important,' said Lord Smog.

'Ah, but they were,' said the witch. 'I found out what you were trying to hide.' She pulled some papers from inside her coat. 'Luckily I looked in old records in the town museum and found a copy of them.'

'Not true,' yelled Lord Smog.

The witch held them up. 'The last owners of this land sold it to the town

council with a binding law that it should never be built on. It should be place for the people of the town.'

'Hoooooooray,' cheered the people in the crowd, enjoying themselves.

'You and the mayor deliberately tried to hide the truth,' said the witch. 'Police! Arrest these men.'

The crowd booed Lord Smog and the mayor again. Then the witch held the loudhailer up one last time. 'It's thanks to these children this land has been saved. It shall always be for the people. A small, wild, green space in the heart of this town.'

Chapter 13
Return to the Wilderness

'CAW! CAW! CAW!'

Willow crawled with Freddie into the Holloway, the tunnel of brambles and thorns. The secret entrance to the Wilderness.

Above the sky was blue, and golden sunlight filtered down through the leaves. Birdsong fell from the trees. Willow couldn't wait to join the others at River Camp.

'Have you heard?' said Fox. 'Lord Smog has had to sell the Wilderness back to the town council. It's going to be left to the wild.'

Raven sighed. 'But Mum says they're going to put some paths through so everyone can come here.'

'It's not such a bad thing,' said Willow. 'If people love the wildlife here, they might want to have more in their own gardens. Besides, one day when we are older, there will be other children who will want to play here too.'

'It's odd to think of the witch as a child,' said Hare.

'Even odder to think of Lord Smog as a boy,' said Bear.

'CAW! CAW!'

The witch's crow flew ahead of her and settled on the top of their den. The witch appeared with a big bag of marshmallows. 'To keep you going now that we can stay here.'

'CAW! CAW!' crowed the crow, bobbing up and down.

'Do the crows really remember?' asked Willow. 'Do they know it was Lord Smog who tried to take eggs from one of their ancestors?'

The witch shrugged her shoulders. 'Who knows. There is so

much we don't know.'

'Like the trees,' said Hare.
'Lord Smog laughed when I said trees could tell if others had been cut down in the forest. It turns out they can tell. They send messages through their roots.'

The witch nodded. 'There is so much more to know. Everything is connected. Let's just hope we look after it long enough to find out.' She stood and looked up at the trees arching overhead. 'Right. I must go. I have a new story to write. I think it might be about some creatures that live together in a woodland.'

'Do they meet monsters?' asked Mouse.
'Maybe,' said the witch.
'Do they find dragons?' asked Fox.
'Lots of dragons,' said the witch.

'Do they have a map?' asked Hare. 'How big is their world?'

'As big as you can imagine it,' said the witch.

'What do they eat?' said Bear.

'Marshmallows of course,' said the witch.

'Are they brave?' asked Raven. 'Are they heroes?'

'They are the best sort of heroes. They are brave and kind, honest and true,' she said. 'And annoying to each other at times,' she added.

Willow wrapped her arms around Freddie on her lap and Sniff curled up at her feet. 'So, what happens in the story?

'Well now,' the witch said, and she smiled. 'That's up to you.'

How to help birds in your garden and outdoor spaces

Make a birdbath

Fresh water is very important for birds—for drinking and bathing. It can be particularly difficult for them to find in cold weather when their usual supply might be frozen, or in hot weather when their usual supply may have dried up.

The easiest way to make sure birds have a water supply is to make them a birdbath. Any shallow dish will work as a birdbath. Something like a large plant pot saucer with a big stone placed in the middle works perfectly, as it gives the birds somewhere to perch.

Make a bird-friendly space

This list of bird-friendly plants will entice a whole host of wildlife to your outdoor space.

- Holly
- Ivy
- Sunflowers
- Hawthorn
- Honeysuckle
- Rowan
- Daisies
- Roses

Make a bird feeder

Birds can experience food shortages at any time of year, so keeping a regular supply of food available to them will really help the birds in your local area. There are lots of foods that birds love, including; sunflower seeds, oatmeal, soaked sultanas, raisins, and currants, mild grated cheese, mealworms, apples and pears cut in half, and bananas and grapes.

Now you know what birds eat, why not try making a bird feeder using the steps below?

You will need:

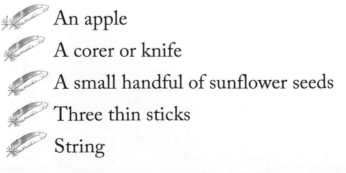 An apple

A corer or knife

A small handful of sunflower seeds

Three thin sticks

String

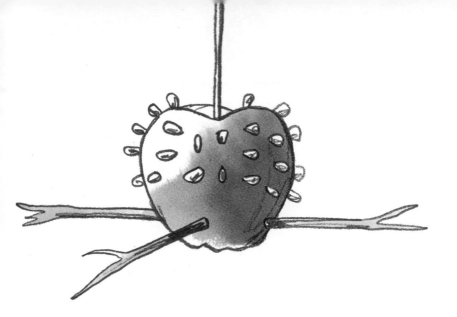

1. Carefully cut the core out of the apple.

2. Push the pointed ends of the sunflower seeds into the top of the apple.

3. Push two of the twigs into the bottom half of the apple to make perches for the birds.

4. Tie your string around the last stick and thread it through the middle of your apple where the core was. The apple should balance on the stick when held up.

5. Your bird feeder is complete. All that's left to do is find somewhere to hang it up!

Gill Lewis spent much of her childhood in the garden, where she ran a small zoo and a veterinary hospital for creepy-crawlies, mice, and birds. When she grew up she became a real vet and travelled from the Arctic to Africa in search of interesting animals and places.

Gill now writes books for children. Her previous novels have published to worldwide critical acclaim and have been translated into more than twenty languages.

She lives in the depths of Somerset with her husband and three children and writes from a tree house in the company of squirrels.

Rebecca Bagley is a children's book illustrator in the south-west of England.

Illustrators are funny sort of grown-ups. They do grown-up things, like brushing their teeth (every day), but they also sit around drawing pictures and then call it a job. Recently, Rebecca has been drawing a lot of leaves, as well as all the magical things that live amongst them, and she couldn't be happier about it.

In between drawings, Rebecca daydreams about having her own garden one day, where she will grow tomatoes, practise handstands, and have a really big dog. Until then, she entertains herself and her little family by feeding new and weird flavours to her baby girl who, so far, has been a very good sport.

Willow Wildthing

Written by Gill Lewis

Willow Wildthing and the Swamp Monster

Illustrated by Rebecca Bagley

Written by Gill Lewis

Willow Wildthing and the Dragon's Egg

Illustrated by Rebecca Bagley

Written by Gill Lewis

Willow Wildthing and the Shooting Star

Illustrated by Rebecca Bagley

Written by Gill Lewis

Willow Wildthing and the Magic Spell

Illustrated by Rebecca Bagley